Printed and Published in Great Britain by D. C. Thomson & Co. Ltd., 185 Fleet Street, London EC4A 2HS. © D. C. Thomson & Co. Ltd., 1996.

ISBN 0-85116-622-9

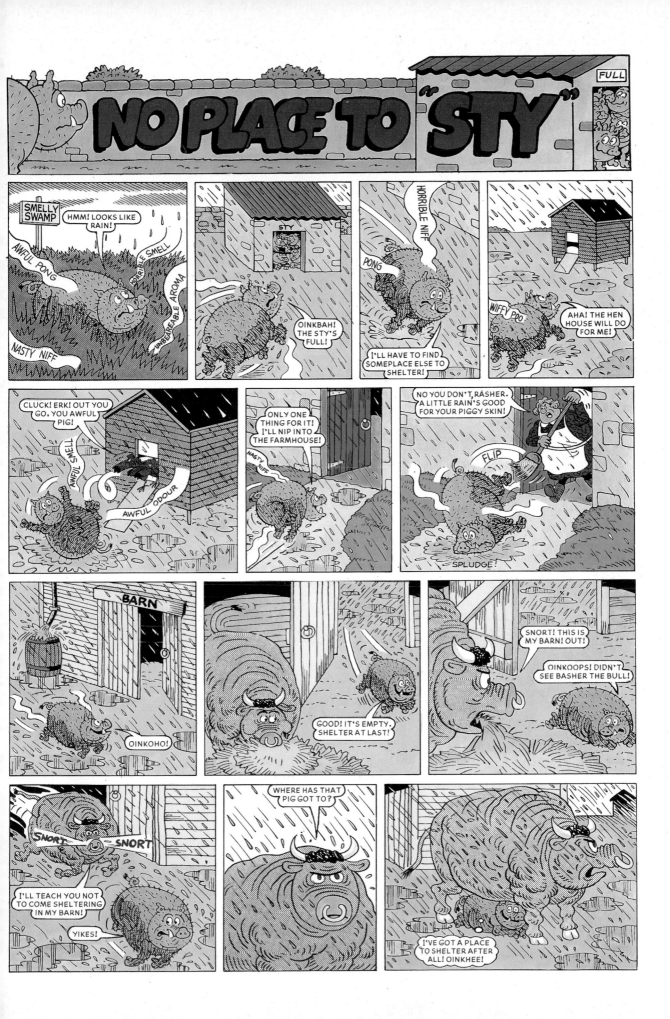

SHEER POETRY

IF –

If you can pelt — and never let
it falter;
If you can soak — and quickly take
your aim;
If you can meet with Bertie and
with Walter
And treat those mincing Softies just
the same;
If you can dodge an unforgiving father
And lose him 'fore the garden's end,
You'll leave him frothing in a lather,
And — which is more —
you'll be a Menace, my friend!

(With apologies to Rudyard Kipling)

PIGSWILL

I wallowed lonely in the mud
Beneath my master's windowsill.
When all at once I heard a thud,
A trough, of rotten veg pigswill.
Turnip halves, old carrot tops,
Potato skins — I scoffed the lot.

I broke wind loudly in the sty,
My trotters 'pon the windowsill.
When all at once I heard a sigh,
It seems I'd made the Menace ill.
For more pigswill, I've dropped big hints,
But now he'll only feed me mints!

(With apologies to William Wordsworth)

GNASHER

Gnasher's gnashers flashing white
At the postie's rear so bright.
What can poor old postie try
To get his trousers home and dry?

Postie! Postie! Running fast,
Gnasher's caught you in at last.
Just give up — you cannot win,
And give us all a great big grin!

(With apologies to William Blake)

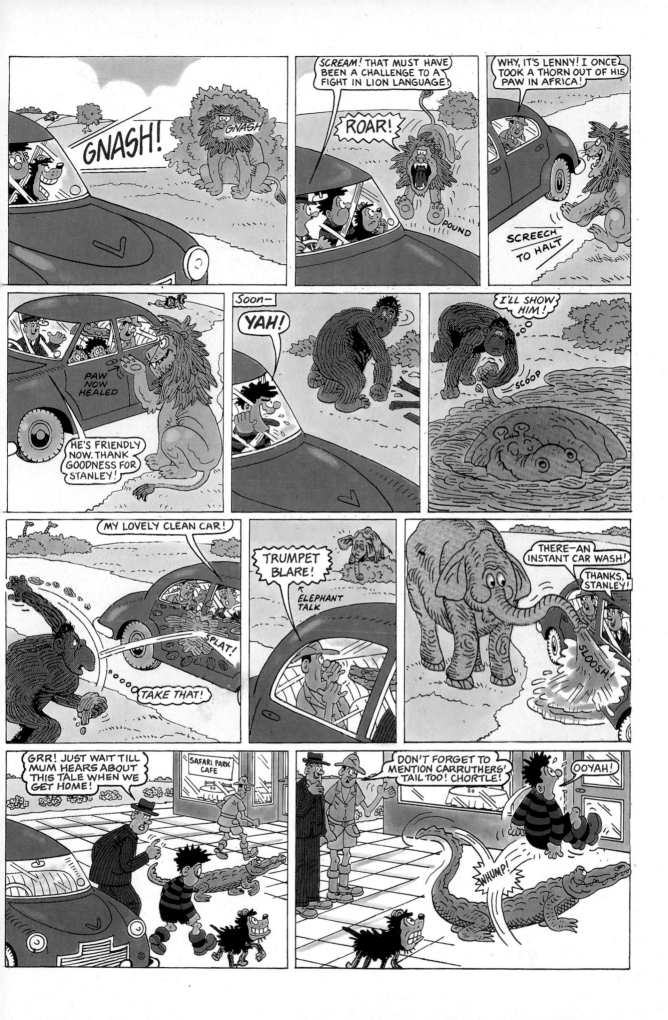

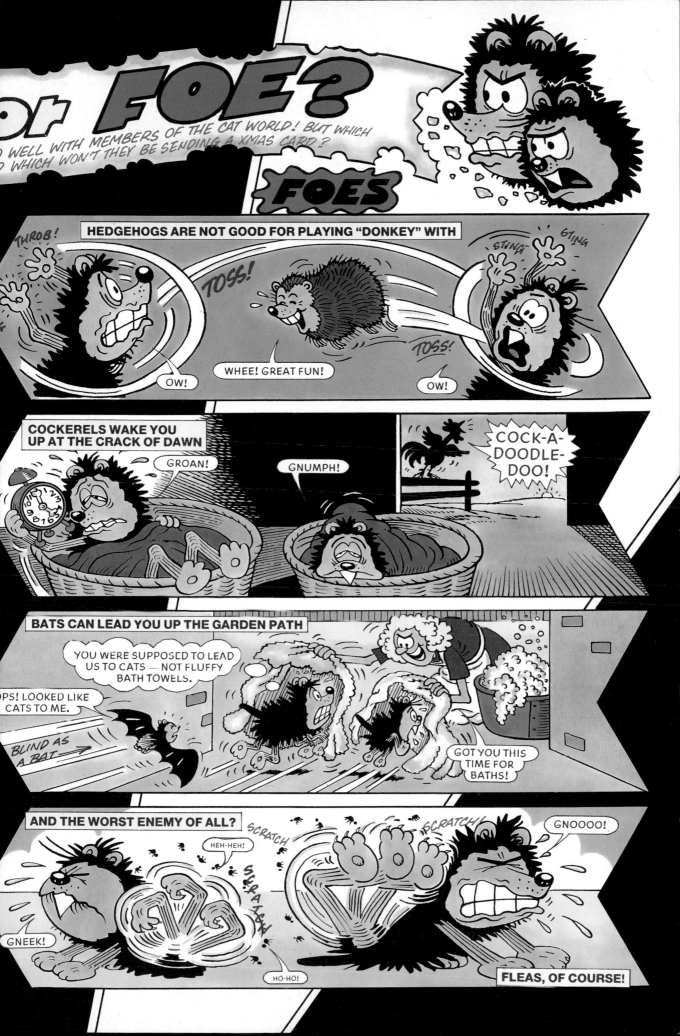

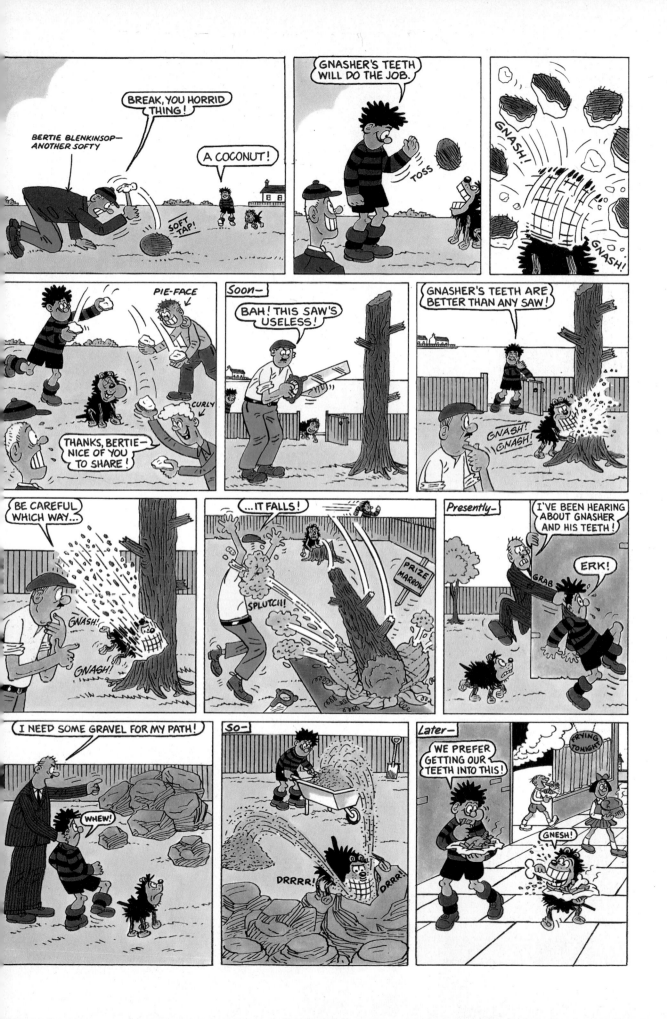

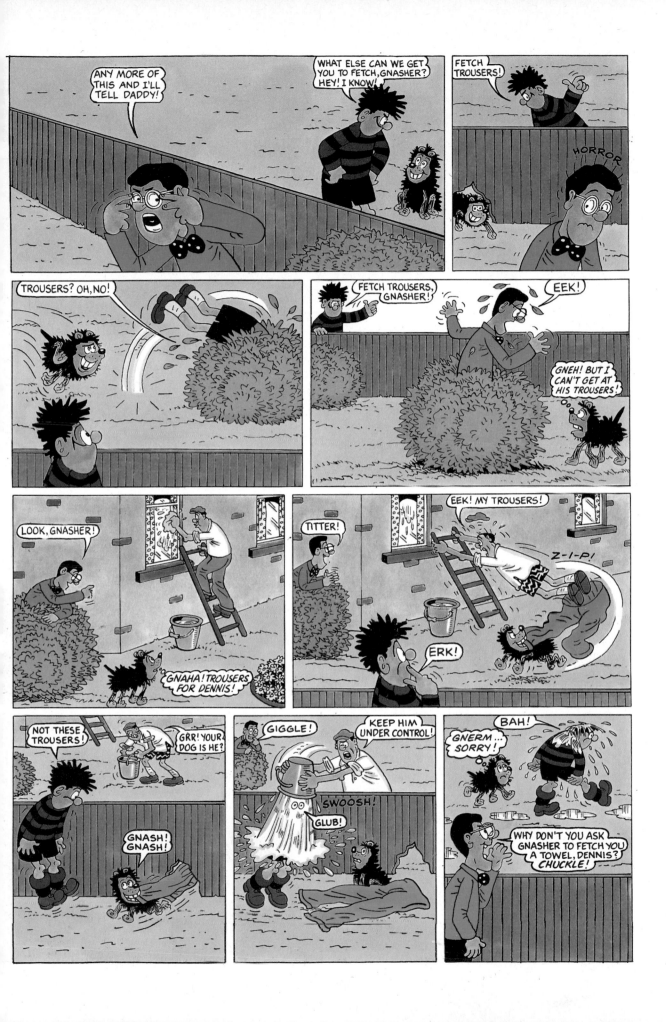

THE MILD

WEST SHOW

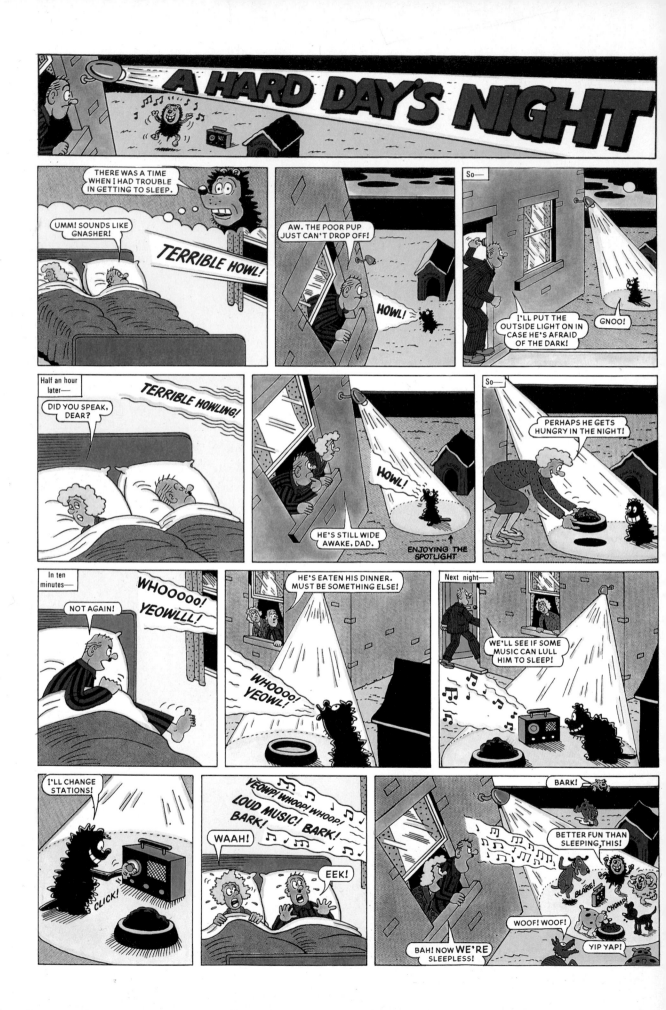

PUP, PUP and AWAY!

IT was to be the coldest night in Beanotown for many a year. It was so cold that Jack Frost was tucked up in his ice house, with frostbite. "It's blooming freezing out there," he said, chillingly.

Gnasher's teeth chattered as he lay in his kennel. "Terrible weather we're having!" said one. "I could do with a dog biscuit," said another. "Shut up!" Gnasher ordered his choppers. The biting wind howled in through the cracks in his kennel and Gnasher howled out through the cracks in his lips. He hadn't been this cold since he swallowed an icicle he'd mistaken for a bone.

At that moment, the wind reached full strength (it had been working out in the gym) and Gnasher and his kennel were swept into the air. Gnasher was terrified . . . GRROWL! (Okay, okay! Gnasher was only slightly worried — Editor) as the wind bore him and his kennel out to sea.

All the creatures of the
deep were amazed as the
kennel flew past and
shouted their greetings to
Gnasher. A dogfish threw
him a bone for breakfast
and even the waves waved.

ZOOM!

GRAB

GNASHER

WAVE

FLIP

WAVE

WHEEE!

GNASHER

SHAVE

BZZZZ!

Gnasher was still cold, so he
had a heated conversation
with a seagull. When the
conversation started to get
out of hand, they decided to
shake and make up.
Gnasher quite liked shaking
— it kept him warm. But he
did look pretty stupid with
make up on.

By now the wind was
dropping faster than a
toothless man with laryngitis
could say, "Two tickets to
Tooting"! Within eight hours
it died away completely!

The kennel floated
gently down on to a strange
tropical beach of purple and
yellow sand. Gnasher was
covered in a strange
mixture of both. "I've been
marooned!" he said. "Is this
island uninhabited or does
nobody live here?" he
wondered. As if in answer to
his question, a familiar smell
reached his nostrils.
(actually, it reached his tail
first and had to ask a flea for
directions).

WHEEE!

GNASHER

FLUMP

"Gnippee! I smell postmen!" Gnasher set off down the beach like a greyhound. He couldn't keep up the impersonation however and ran on like the Wire-haired Abyssinian Tripe Hound he really was.

A fabulous sight greeted Gnasher's eyes. "Hello, Gnasher's eyes!" it said. As far as his ears could see, the beach was covered by sunbathing posties.

"I've found the legendary lost island of retired postmen!" Gnasher was filling up with excitement. (There was a handy self-service "excitement" station nearby).

Eventually, he fell into a deep, contented sleep and dreamt of doing it all again tomorrow. The posties had other ideas!

TWANG!
Gnasher was fired into the air and was caught by the wind. (It had been learning cricket as well as working out in the gym).

The wind carried the sleeping Gnasher back to Beanotown, back to the Menace house and in through Dennis' bedroom window.

After a few gallons of lead-free five star excitement, he dived into the middle of a group of panicking posties! Nipping a rear here, biting a trouser leg there, he ran himself off his feet, his ankles and his knees chasing them across the beach.

They picked up the slumbering Gnasher and placed him on the end of a palm tree they had bent back to form a catapult . . .

When Gnasher woke up in the morning, he thought he'd been dreaming, but no-one ever did explain what happened to his kennel or why he had a lovely sun tan in the middle of January!

DENNIS' DEPARTMENT STORE

WHAT EVERY MENACE AND THEIR FAMILY WANT

SECOND FLOOR   COSMETICS

DO I LOOK GOOD, DENNIS?

DAB

JUST GREAT, WALTER!

FACE PAINTS

I'LL PRETEND I'M NOT DENNIS' DAD AND RUN AWAY!

STICK

GLUE

DISGUISE MAKE-UP

AND EASIER TO ESCAPE TRIMMING. GNEE-HEE!

ZOO

THIS WILL MAKE IT EASIER TO CUT!

SHAVING FOAM FOR TRIMMING DOG HAIR

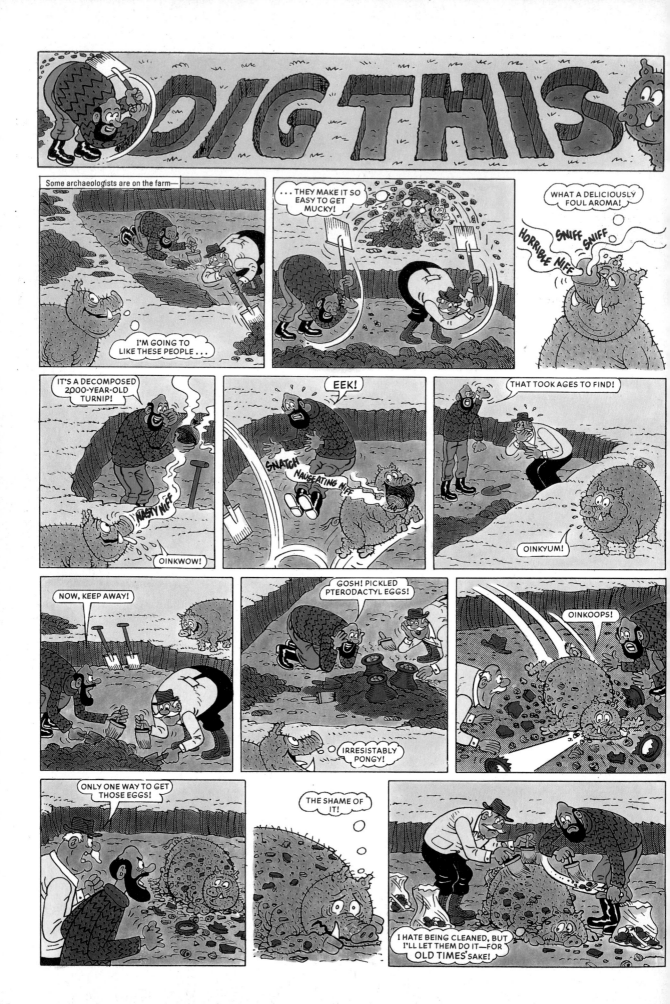

GNURSERY RHYMES

PAT-A-CAKE, PAT-A-CAKE,
DEAR OLD MUM.
BAKE ME A CAKE, GO ON,
BE A CHUM.
PAT IT AND PRICK IT AND
PILE ON THICK CREAM.
I'LL GIVE IT TO WALTER
WHO'S LIKELY TO SCREAM.

SIMPLE SIMON MET A PIE MAN
GOING TO THE FAIR.
SAID SIMPLE SIMON TO THE PIE MAN,
"LET ME TASTE YOUR WARE."
SAID THE PIE MAN TO SIMPLE SIMON,
"THE TRADE'S BEEN REALLY BUZZIN'!
PIE FACE BOUGHT UP ALL MY PIES –
HE'S SCOFFED AROUND EIGHT DOZEN!"